FROM WHEAT
To Pasta

A Photo Essay
by Robert Egan

Children's Press

A Division of Grolier Publishing
New York London Hong Kong Sydney
Danbury, Connecticut

Created and Developed by The Learning Source

Designed by Josh Simons

Acknowledgement: We would like to thank the many people and organizations who provided technical assistance with this project, with special thanks to the people from Raffetto's pasta. Their help is greatly appreciated.

Photo Credits: Bernard Anderson for North Dakota Wheat Commission: 8-9; Kansas State University Department of Communications: 10-12; Kansas Wheat Commission: 16,17, back cover; Norma Anderson for North Dakota Wheat Commission: 2; North Dakota Mill & Elevator: 13,14,15; Robert Egan: cover (inset); 4-7, 30-32: Robert Egan for Raffetto's Pasta Company: 18-25; 27-29; Robert Egan for Tutta Pasta: 26 (top); Wheat Foods Council: 1,3.

Note: The actual pasta-making process often varies from manufacturer to manufacturer. The facts and details included in this book are representative of one of the most common ways of producing pasta today.

1 2 3 4 5 6 7 8 9 10 R 06 05 04 03 02 01 00 99 98 97

Library of Congress Catalonging-in-Publication Data
Egan, Robert. 1953-
    From Wheat to Pasta : a photo essay / by Robert Egan.
    p.   cm. — (Changes)
    Summary: Describes, in text and photographs, the steps in making various kinds of pasta from growing and harvesting the wheat through the grinding of the flour to making the dough and shaping the final product.
    ISBN 0-516-20709-1   (ISBN 0-516-26069-3 pbk.)
    1. Pasta products——Juvenile literature. [1. Pasta products.]
I. Title. II. Series: Changes (New York, N.Y.)
TP435.M3E38 1997
664'.755—dc21,   96-39302
                                                        CIP
                                                        AC

Pasta!

Scoop it up . . .

. . . or slurp it down.

Paste it into a picture . . .

. . . or wear it to a party.

Pasta!

It's more than just food.

But where does pasta come from?

It starts out as golden wheat, growing in the sun.

At harvest time, a huge machine called a combine comes along and cuts the wheat.

Off come the stalks, and tiny kernels flow into the truck.

The kernels are stored in tall, round grain elevators . . .

. . . until they go to a flour mill. Here, the kernels are cleaned and sorted.

Next, a tempering machine soaks the kernels, making them easier to grind.

Then big roller mills crack and grind the kernels into a grainy powder.

The powder gets sifted, ground, and cleaned until . . .

. . . it finally becomes pure, silky flour. Now the flour is on its way—down long chutes into cloth sacks . . .

. . . down even more chutes and onto trains, trucks, or barges such as this one.

At last the flour ends up in the hands of a pasta maker.

He dumps the flour
into a bin . . .

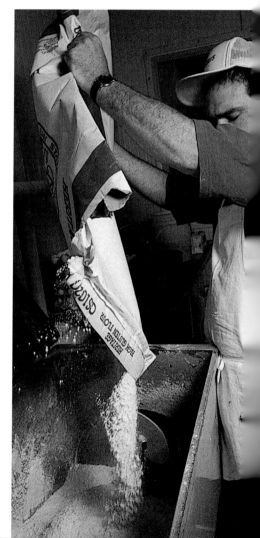

. . . and mixes it with water.

Most pasta is just flour and water. But sometimes other ingredients are added, such as yellow eggs, green spinach, or red tomatoes.

Then it's on to the kneading machine, where the flour is punched and stretched and rolled. In goes the flour mixture. Out comes . . .

. . . a long, folded sheet of dough.

The dough is rolled again and again, thinner and thinner.

It is laid out on a table.

The long ribbons of pasta dough are cut into sheets and set aside. What do you think went into the dough to make it so green?

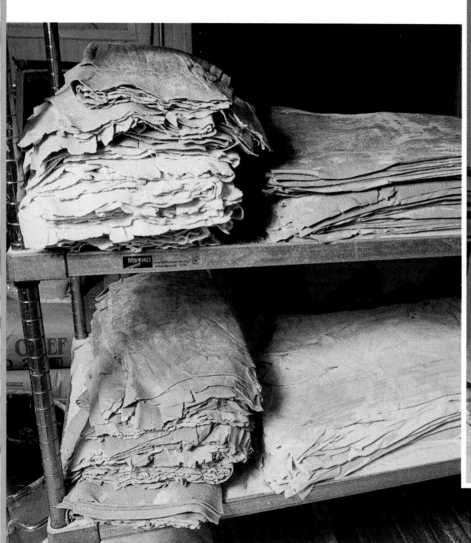

Now it's ready to be shaped. This machine is cutting long, thin strips of pasta.

Other machines, called extruders, create short, fat pasta tubes,

or little pasta wheels.

Finally, the pasta is packed in boxes . . .

27

. . . and sent off to stores, where it waits for you.

Now all you have to do is cook it in boiling water. Then add some sauce, and eat all you want.

Sometimes it's a bit messy.
But don't worry. After all . . .

. . . it's pasta!

Here are a few of the many different types of pasta.
What other kinds can you name?

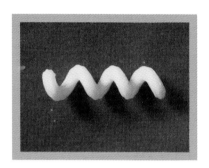

Fusilli (few SEEL lee) is also called corkscrew pasta.

Farfalle (far FAHL leh), or butterfly pasta, is sometimes called bowtie pasta.

Ravioli (rav ee OH lee) are stuffed with lots of different fillings.

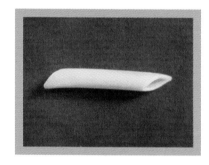

Penne (PEN neh) means old-fashioned feather pens in Italian.

Radiatore (rah dee a TOR eh) means radiator in italian.

Rotelle (roh TEL leh) are also called wagon wheels.